Who Likes Rain?

Wong Herbert Yee

Henry Holt and Company • New York

For Christy

Henry Holt and Company, LLC, *Publishers since 1866*
175 Fifth Avenue, New York, New York 10010
www.henryholtchildrensbooks.com

Henry Holt® is a registered trademark of Henry Holt and Company, LLC.
Copyright © 2007 by Wong Herbert Yee
All rights reserved. Distributed in Canada by H. B. Fenn and Company Ltd.

Library of Congress Cataloging-in-Publication Data
Yee, Wong Herbert. Who likes rain? / Wong Herbert Yee.—1st ed.
p.   cm.
Summary: As a young girl splashes in the rain, she plays a guessing game
with the reader about other living things that enjoy a cloudburst.
ISBN-13: 978-0-8050-7734-6 / ISBN-10: 0-8050-7734-0
[1. Rain and rainfall—Fiction. 2. Guessing games—Fiction. 3. Stories in rhyme.] I. Title.
PZ8.3.Y42Who 2006   [E]—dc22   2006003429

First Edition—2007 / Designed by Amelia May Anderson
The artist used Prismacolors on Arches watercolor paper to create
the illustrations for this book.
Printed in China on acid-free paper. ∞

10 9 8 7 6 5 4 3 2 1

Pit-pit-pit on the windowpane.

Down, down, down come the drops of rain.

Who wants rain?

Who needs April showers?

I know who . . .

The trees and the flowers!

Raindrops falling
Down in spring
Hit the awning,
Ping-ping-ping!

When it rains,
Who's the first to scat?
I know! Do you?
Mew, mew . . .

It's the cat!

Gurgle, gurgle
Down the gutters
Out the spout
The water splutters.

Who likes rain?
Not Papa's old truck.
Who likes rain?
Quack, quack . . .

It's a duck!

Pitty-plip-PLOP,
Pitty-pat-SPLAT!
I can catch raindrops
In my hat.

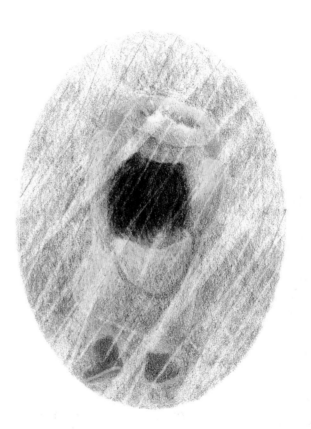

When it rains,
Who comes out to squirm?
I know! Do you?
Creep, creep . . .

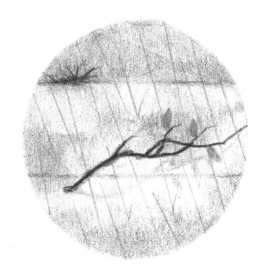

It's a worm!

Raindrops beat like a tom-tom drum
On my umbrella, *rum-a-tum-tum!*

Who likes rain?
Not my neighbor's dog.
Who likes rain?
Croak, croak . . .

It's a frog!

A wind comes *whooshing*
Through the trees.
It shakes the raindrops
From the leaves.

Who likes rain?
It jumps with a *splish!*
I know! Do you?
Glub, glub . . .

It's a fish!

After a while the showers stop.
A few last drops fall, *plip-plip—PLOP!*
Clouds break up, no need to huddle.
All that's left is . . .

. . . one BIG puddle.

Who likes rain even more than a duck?

More than a frog in the muckety-muck?

Who needs rain besides trees and flowers?

Who wants a day with April showers?

Off comes the raincoat,

boots, and hat.

Who likes rain?

I do!

KER-*SPLAT!*